THE LITTLE BOOK OF
MARK TWAIN

First published in 2022 by OH!
An Imprint of Welbeck Non-Fiction Limited,
part of Welbeck Publishing Group.
Based in London and Sydney.
www.welbeckpublishing.com

Compilation text © Welbeck Non-Fiction Limited 2022
Design © Welbeck Non-Fiction Limited 2022

ISBN 978-1-80069-195-7

Compiled and written by: Stella Caldwell
Project manager: Russell Porter
Design: Tony Seddon
Production: Jess Brisley

A CIP catalogue record for this book is available from the British Library

Printed in China

10 9 8 7 6 5 4 3 2 1

THE LITTLE BOOK OF
MARK TWAIN

ADVENTURES FROM THE
FATHER OF AMERICAN LITERATURE

CONTENTS

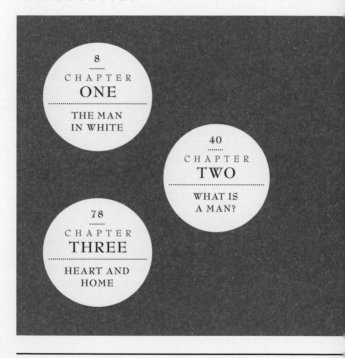

INTRODUCTION

"All modern American literature comes from one book by Mark Twain called *Huckleberry Finn*."

So said Ernest Hemingway in 1935, thus sealing the reputation of Samuel Langhorne Clemens—better known by his pen name, Mark Twain—as the "father of American literature." Twain's masterpiece about boyhood life on the Mississippi River, and its predecessor, *The Adventures of Tom Sawyer*, combined humor, warmth, and superb storytelling to vividly reflect the American way of life in the second half of the nineteenth century.

In *Huckleberry Finn*, Twain broke with the idea that literature should be written in "literary English," instead telling Huck's story in the colorful voice of a poor, uneducated American boy. This groundbreaking experiment with the vernacular inspired writers around the world, while the novel's insights into race, slavery, and moral issues continue to be relevant today.

But Twain was much more than a superb novelist. He was an accomplished raconteur, journalist, social critic, and humorist—and, of course, he was a travel writer. It is fascinating to know that Twain's account of his journey to Europe and the Middle East, *The Innocents Abroad*, was the most celebrated of his books in his lifetime. In 1867, he wrote, "I am wild with impatience to move—move—Move!" And move he did, crossing the Atlantic 29 times, living in several European cities, and circumnavigating the globe.

For all his adventures and literary success, however, Twain's personal life was marred by tragedy. Poor financial judgments brought him to near bankruptcy, and the early deaths of three of his four children were devastating blows. But throughout his turbulent life, he never lost his love of words or his readiness to express an opinion.

Brimming with Twain's humor, ideas, and views, this volume features some of the author's best-loved sayings alongside extracts from his writings and fascinating facts about his life. It is a celebration of the man, his character, and his incredible talent.

CHAPTER
ONE

THE MAN IN WHITE

Twain once observed, "All life demands change, variety, contrast—else there is small zest to it." From his Mississippi River boyhood through to his worldwide travels and emergence as a global celebrity, the writer certainly lived a full and rich life.

In the following quotes, Twain, and those who knew him best, reflect on the man behind the white suit.

"We were good boys, good Presbyterian boys, and loyal and all that; anyway, we were good Presbyterian boys when the weather was doubtful; when it was fair, we did wander a little from the fold."

67th birthday dinner, November 28, 1902

"Next after fine colors, I like plain white. One of my sorrows, when the summer ends, is that I must put off my cheery and comfortable white clothes and enter for the winter into the depressing captivity of the shapeless and degrading black ones."

Autobiography of Mark Twain, 2010

"I am a border-ruffian from the State of Missouri. I am a Connecticut Yankee by adoption. In me, you have Missouri morals, Connecticut culture; this, gentlemen, is the combination which makes the perfect man."

Plymouth Rock and the Pilgrims speech,
December 22, 1881

Mark Twain was born as Samuel Langhorne Clemens in the tiny town of Florida, Missouri, on November 30, 1835.

He was the sixth of seven children—four of whom died in childhood—and grew into a frail, sickly child.

When he was four, the family moved to the town of Hannibal on the Mississippi River—which would later be immortalized as the town of St. Petersburg in Twain's stories.

"When I was a boy, there was but one permanent ambition among my comrades in our village on the west bank of the Mississippi River. That was, to be a steamboat man."

Life on the Mississippi, 1883

Illustration from *Life on the Mississippi*, 1883

"I have always been able to gain my living without doing any work; for the writing of books and magazine matter was always play, not work. I enjoyed it; it was merely billiards to me."

Mark Twain in Eruption, 1940

"Twain was so good with crowds that he became, in competition with singers and dancers and actors and acrobats, one of the most popular performers of his time."

Kurt Vonnegut, Jr., *The Unabridged Mark Twain*, 1976

"I love to hear myself talk, because I get so much instruction and moral upheaval out of it."

Autobiography of Mark Twain, 2010

"The story of my life will make certain people sit up and take notice, but I will use my influence not to have it published until the persons mentioned in it and their children and grandchildren are dead. I tell you, it will be something awful. It will be what you might call good reading."

In an interview aboard *SS Minneapolis*,
New York, June 8, 1907

Twain claimed he gained his love of storytelling from his gentle, loving mother, Jane.

His strict, austere father, John, was a lawyer and storekeeper. His death, when Twain was 11 years old, pushed the family into poverty.

Forced to leave school and start work, Twain became a printer's apprentice and was soon writing occasional articles for a newspaper owned by his brother Orion.

"**A**n author values a compliment even when it comes from a source of doubtful competency."

Mark Twain in Eruption, 1940

"What a wee little part of a person's life are his acts and his words! His real life is led in his head and is known to none but himself. All day long, and every day, the mill of his brain is grinding and his thoughts, not those other things are his history … The mass of him is hidden—it and its volcanic fires that toss and boil, and never rest, night nor day."

Clara Clemens (Twain's daughter),
Mark Twain at Your Fingertips, 2009

"Sometimes my feelings are so hot that I have to take to the pen and pour them out on paper to keep them from setting me afire inside; then all that ink and labor are wasted, because I can't print the result. I have just finished an article of this kind, and it satisfies me entirely. It does my weather-beaten soul good to read it, and admire the trouble it would make for me and the family."

"The Privilege of the Grave," written in 1905 but published for the first time in the *New Yorker*, 2008

"When a man loves cats, I am his friend and comrade, without further introduction."

"An Incident," *Who Is Mark Twain?*, 2009

"To my mind Mark Twain was beyond question the largest man of his time, both in the direct outcome of his work and more important still, if possible, in his indirect influence as a protesting force in an age of iron philistinism."

Rudyard Kipling, in a letter, 1935

"**I**t is from experiences such as mine that we get our education of life. We string them into jewels or into tinware, as we may choose."

Mark Twain, A Biography,
Albert Bigelow Paine, 1912

Growing up by the Mississippi River, Twain longed to become a steamboat pilot.

His dream was realized when he became a pilot's apprentice at the age of 21, gaining his license two years later.

His piloting career was cut short in 1861, however, when the start of the civil war disrupted riverboat traffic.

Illustration from *Life on the Mississippi,* 1883

"I wish I was back there piloting up & down the river again. Verily, all is vanity and little worth—save piloting."

In a letter to his mother, Jane Clemens, October 1865

"All modern American literature comes from one book by Mark Twain called *Huckleberry Finn*. American writing comes from that. There is nothing before. There has been nothing as good since."

Ernest Hemingway on Twain, *Green Hills of Africa*, 1935

"You don't know about me, without you have read a book by the name of 'The Adventures of Tom Sawyer'; but that ain't no matter. That book was made by Mr. Mark Twain, and he told the truth, mainly. There was things which he stretched, but mainly he told the truth."

The Adventures of Huckleberry Finn, 1884

Illustration from *Huckleberry Finn*, 1884

"My description is as follows: Born 1835; 5 ft. 8½ inches tall; weight about 145 pounds … dark brown hair and red moustache, full face with very high ears and light grey beautiful beaming eyes and a damned good moral character."

Application for a German passport, 1878

"Ah, well, I am a great and sublime fool. But then I am God's fool, and all his works must be contemplated with respect."

Letter to William Dean Howells, 1877

"I feel the twinkle of his eye in his handshake. He makes you feel his heart is a tender Iliad of human sympathy."

Helen Keller on Twain, *The Story of My Life*, 1903

"Papa, the way things are going, pretty soon there won't be anybody left for you to get acquainted with but God."

Jean Clemens (Mark Twain's daughter),
Mark Twain's Notebook, 1933

"I lay awake all last night aggravating myself with this prospect of seeing my hated nom de plume (for I do loathe the very sight of it) in print again every month."

Letter to Orion Clemens, March 11, 1871

"The 20th century is a stranger to me—I wish it well but my heart is all for my own century. I took 65 years of it, just on a risk, but if I had known as much about it as I know now I would have taken the whole of it."

Mark Twain's Notebook, 1933

CHAPTER
TWO

WHAT IS
A MAN?

In 1906, Twain's essay "What is a Man?"
roamed over the moral, religious, and
philosophical questions of the day to give
a somewhat dark picture of human
nature.

An astute observer of people, the author's
writing was often concerned with the
drama, comedy, and tragedy behind even
the "dullest exterior."

"It is a pathetic thought. We struggle, we rise, we tower in the zenith a brief and gorgeous moment, with the adoring eyes of the nations upon us, then the lights go out, oblivion closes around us, our glory fades and vanishes, a few generations drift by, and naught remains but a mystery and a name."

"The Secret History of Eddypus,"
Mark Twain's Fables of Man, 1972

"This curious & pathetic fact of life: that when parents are old & their children grown up, the grown-up children are not the persons they formerly were; that their former selves have wandered away, never to return again, save in dream-glimpses of their young forms that tarry a moment & gladden the eye, then vanish & break the heart."

Memorial to Susy Clemens (Twain's daughter, who died at the age of 24), 1896

As a child, Twain witnessed violence and death on several occasions. He discovered a corpse in his father's office—belonging to an emigrant who had been stabbed in a fight—and on another occasion, saw a man murdered in the street.

When he was 11, a friend drowned before his eyes and days later, he discovered the mutilated body of a drowned slave.

"Always avoid violence; in this age of charity and kindliness, the time has gone by for such things. Leave dynamite to the low and unrefined."

"Advice to Youth," May 15, 1882

"Always do right. This will gratify some people and astonish the rest."

Note to the Young People's Society, Greenpoint Presbyterian Church, 1901

"**M**an is the only animal that blushes. Or needs to."

Following the Equator, 1897

"One cannot have everything the way he would like it. A man has no business to be depressed by a disappointment, anyway; he ought to make up his mind to get even."

A Connecticut Yankee in King Arthur's Court, 1889

The author dreamt up his pen
name during his time as a
steamboat pilot on the Mississippi.
"Mark Twain" was a boatman's call
meaning the river was two fathoms
deep, the minimum depth for safe
riverboat navigation.

It wasn't Twain's first pseudonym
though—his earliest efforts were
written under the names "Josh" and
"Thomas Jefferson Snodgrass."

"Everyone is a moon, and has a dark side which he never shows to anybody."

Following the Equator, 1897

"It was only a little thing to do, and no trouble; and it's the little things that smooths people's roads the most..."

The Adventures of Huckleberry Finn, 1884

“Human beings can be awful cruel to one another.”

The Adventures of Huckleberry Finn, 1884

"All say, 'How hard it is that we have to die'—a strange complaint to come from the mouths of people who have had to live."

Pudd'nhead Wilson, 1894

In 1858, Twain's younger brother, Henry—a trainee steamboat pilot—was horribly burned in a steamboat boiler explosion and later died from his injuries.

Twain had persuaded his brother to take up the role and felt guilty for the rest of his life.

Shortly after his death, he wrote in a letter, "My poor Henry—my darling, my pride, my glory… O, God! This is hard to bear".

"Of course, no man is entirely in his right mind at any time."

The Mysterious Stranger, 1916

"Miss Watson, a tolerable slim old maid, with goggles on … told me all about the bad place, and I said I wished I was there. She got mad then, but I didn't mean no harm. All I wanted was to go somewheres; all I wanted was a change, I warn't particular. She said it was wicked to say what I said; said she wouldn't say it for the whole world; she was going to live so as to go to the good place. Well, I couldn't see no advantage in going where she was going, so I made up my mind I wouldn't try for it."

Huck on heaven and hell,
Adventures of Huckleberry Finn, 1884

"The elastic heart of youth cannot be compressed into one constrained shape long at a time."

The Adventures of Tom Sawyer, 1876

Illustration from *The Adventures of Tom Sawyer*, 1876

Twain was an ardent lover
of cats and owned up to 19 of them
at one time.

He enjoyed their company so much
that he even rented kittens on some
of his travels. Here are just a few
of their names:

Apollinaris	Tammany
Beelzebub	Zoroaster
Buffalo Bill	Soapy Sal
Sour Mash	Pestilence

"Of all God's creatures there is only one that cannot be made the slave of the lash. That one is the cat. If man could be crossed with the cat it would improve man, but it would deteriorate the cat."

Notebook, 1894

"Right is right, and wrong is wrong, and a body ain't got no business doing wrong when he ain't ignorant and knows better."

The Adventures of Huckleberry Finn, 1884

Illustration from *Huckleberry Finn*, 1884

"Of all the creatures that were made, man is the most detestable. Of the entire brood he is the only one—the solitary one—that possesses malice. That is the basest of all instincts, passions, vices—the most hateful. He is the only creature that has pain for sport, knowing it to be pain."

Autobiography of Mark Twain, 2010

"Now and then we had a hope that if we lived and were good, God would permit us to be pirates."

Life on the Mississippi, 1883

"Humor is mankind's greatest blessing."

Mark Twain, A Biography, Albert Bigelow Paine, 1912

"Training is everything. The peach was once a bitter almond; cauliflower is nothing but cabbage with a college education."

Pudd'nhead Wilson, 1894

"Courage is resistance to fear, mastery of fear—not absence of fear. Except a creature be part coward, it is not a compliment to say he is brave; it is merely a loose misapplication of the word."

Pudd'nhead Wilson, 1894

The first literary hit of Twain's
career was a story called
"The Celebrated Jumping Frog of
Calaveras County." The amusing
tale of a gambler who would bet on
anything, it was meant to be
published in a friend's book, but
Twain was late in submitting it.

The story was sent to the *New
York Saturday Press*, where
its publication, in 1875, brought
Twain widespread acclaim.

"The man who is born stingy can be taught to give liberally— with his hands; but not with his heart. The man born kind and compassionate can have that disposition crushed down out of sight by embittering experience; but if it were an organ, the postmortem would find it in his corpse."

Christian Science, 1907

"The common eye sees only the outside of things, and judges by that, but the seeing eye pierces through and reads the heart and the soul, finding there capacities which the outside didn't indicate or promise, and which the other kind couldn't detect."

Personal Recollections of Joan of Arc, 1896

"To be envied is the human being's chiefest joy."

The Mysterious Stranger, 1916

"**S**trip the human race, absolutely naked, and it would be a real democracy. But the introduction of even a rag of tiger skin, or a cowtail, could make a badge of distinction and be the beginning of a monarchy."

Mark Twain's Notebook, 1933

"We are always more anxious to be distinguished for a talent which we do not possess, than to be praised for the fifteen which we do possess."

Autobiography of Mark Twain, 2010

"The Impartial Friend: Death, the only immortal who treats us all alike, whose pity and whose peace and whose refuge are for all—the soiled and the pure, the rich and the poor, the loved and the unloved."

Last written statement, *Moments with Mark Twain*, Albert Bigelow Paine, 1920

CHAPTER
THREE

HEART AND HOME

Twain adored his wife, Livy, and his life
was enriched by family and friendships.

However, the tragic deaths of three
of his four children brought intense
pain and grief. The fragility of life
and personal happiness is a theme that
haunts much of the author's writing.

"This 4th of February will be the mightiest day in the history of our lives, the holiest, & the most generous toward us both—for it makes of two fractional lives a whole; it gives to two purposeless lives a work, & doubles the strength of each whereby to perform it; it gives to two questioning natures a reason for living, & something to live for."

Letter to Olivia Langdon a few months
before their marriage, September 8, 1869

"True love is the only heart disease that is best left to 'run on'—the only affection of the heart for which there is no help, and none desired."

Mark Twain's Notebook, 1933

Twain met his future wife, Olivia—or Livy—after he and her brother became friends while traveling to Europe and the Middle East aboard a steamship, in 1867.

Back in the U.S., Twain was introduced to Olivia in New York— on their first date, the pair went to see the author Charles Dickens give one of his famous readings.

They were married in 1870.

"I—well I was an exception, you understand—my kind don't turn up every day. We are very rare. We are a sort of human century plant, and we don't blossom in everybody's front yard."

In a letter to his wife, Olivia, September 8, 1869

"The course of free love never runs smooth. I suppose we have all tried it."

Notebook, 1904

"People talk about beautiful friendships between two persons of the same sex. What is the best of that sort, as compared with the friendship of man and wife, where the best impulses and highest ideals of both are the same. There is no place for comparison between the two friendships; the one is earthly, the other divine."

A Connecticut Yankee in King Arthur's Court, 1889

Illustration from *A Connecticut Yankee in King Arthur's Court*, 1889

HEART AND HOME

"An enemy can partly ruin a man, but it takes a good-natured injudicious friend to complete the thing and make it perfect."

Pudd'nhead Wilson, 1894

"After all these years, I see that I was mistaken about Eve in the beginning; it is better to live outside the Garden with her than inside it without her."

Extracts From Adam's Diary, 1904

Twain's five-month trip to the Mediterranean, aboard the *USS Quaker City*, gave rise to his great travel book *The Innocents Abroad*.

Published in 1869, the book presented vivid and often humorous views of places such as Marseilles, Rome, and Damascus.

A huge success, it remained the bestselling of all Twain's books in his lifetime.

Illustration from *The Innocents Abroad,* 1897

"Love seems the swiftest, but it is the slowest of all growths. No man or woman really knows what perfect love is until they have been married a quarter of a century."

Mark Twain's Notebook, 1933

"What a world of trouble those who never marry escape! There are many happy matches, it is true, and sometimes 'my dear' and 'my love' come from the heart; but what sensible bachelor, rejoicing in his freedom and years of discretion, will run the tremendous risk?"

"Connubial Bliss," *Hannibal Journal*,
4 November 1852

"Good friends, good books
and a sleepy conscience: this is
the ideal life."

Notebook, 1898

"Broad, wholesome, charitable views of men and things cannot be acquired by vegetating in one little corner of the earth all one's lifetime."

The Innocents Abroad

"A very dear little ashcat, but has claws."

On his daughter Clara, letter to Joseph Twichell,
June 24, 1905

"It is one of the mysteries of our nature that a man, all unprepared, can receive a thunder-stroke like that and live. There is but one reasonable explanation of it. The intellect is stunned by the shock and but gropingly gathers the meaning of the words. The power to realize their full import is mercifully lacking."

On the death of his beloved daughter Susy
(at the age of 24),
Autobiography of Mark Twain, 2010

Twain and his wife, Livy, had
one son and three daughters. There are
no living descendants. (Twain's only
grandchild, Nina Gabrilowitsch,
the daughter of his daughter Clara, had
no children.)

Langdon: Died of diphtheria as an infant.

Susy: Twain's clear favorite, she died from
meningitis aged 24.

Clara: Fiercely independent, Twain's third
child was the only one to survive him.

Jean: Died from drowning, aged 29,
after having a seizure in a bath.

"A family brought love, and distributed it among many objects, and intensified it, and this engendered wearing cares and anxieties, and when the objects suffered or died the miseries and anxieties multiplied and broke the heart and shortened life..."

The Mysterious Stranger, 1916

"I remember those days of twenty-one years ago, and a certain pathos clings about them. Susy, with her manifold young charms and her iridescent mind, was as lovely a bubble as any we made that day—and as transitory. She passed, as they passed, in her youth and beauty, and nothing of her is left but a heartbreak and a memory."

Remembering his daughter Susy,
Autobiography of Mark Twain, 2010

"When you fish for love, bait
with your heart, not your brain."

Notebook, 1898

"Love is a madness; if thwarted it develops fast."

"The Memorable Assassination,"
What is Man? And Other Essays, 1917

"Marriage—yes, it is the supreme felicity of life. I concede it. And it is also the supreme tragedy of life. The deeper the love the surer the tragedy. And the more disconsolating when it comes."

In a letter to Father Fitz-Simon, June 5, 1908

TRAMPING AROUND THE WORLD

In 1867, Twain wrote to his mother,
"I am impatient to move—move—*Move!*"

It reflected his great hunger to see and
experience new things—indeed, for much
of his career, he spent a surprising amount
of time living or traveling abroad.

Today, Twain is best remembered for his
fiction—but it was his travel writing, and
particularly *The Innocents Abroad*, that
brought him fame in his time.

"There is no unhappiness like the misery of sighting land (and work) again after a cheerful, careless voyage."

In a letter to Will Bowen, 1866

"France has neither winter
nor summer nor morals—apart
from these drawbacks it is a
fine country."

Mark Twain's Notebook, 1933

"**I** have found out that there ain't no surer way to find out whether you like people or hate them than to travel with them."

Tom Sawyer Abroad, 1894

Twain first laid eyes on the "new-fangled typing machine" in the 1870s.

He found the typewriter to be "full of caprices, full of defects—devilish ones," but he went on to write *Life on the Mississippi* (1883) on one.

It was the first literary work to be completed on such a machine.

"If ze zhentlemans will to me make ze grande honneur to me rattain in hees serveece, I shall show to him every sing zat is magnifique to look upon in ze beautiful Parree. I speaky ze Angleesh pairfaitemaw."

The Innocents Abroad, 1869

Illustration from *The Innocents Abroad*, 1897

"The full moon was riding high in the cloudless heavens now. We sauntered carelessly and unthinkingly to the edge of the lofty battlements of the citadel, and looked down, and, lo! a vision! And such a vision! Athens by moonlight! All the beauty in all the world could not rival it!"

On Athens, The American Vandal Speech, 1868–69

"I don't believe there is anything in the whole earth that you can't learn in Berlin except the German language.**"**

Mark Twain's Notebook, 1933

"There are many humorous things in the world; among them, the white man's notion that he is less savage than the other savages."

Following the Equator, 1897

"In early times some sufferer had to sit up with a toothache, and he put in the time inventing the German language.**"**

Mark Twain's Notebook, 1933

The Adventures of Tom Sawyer
was published in 1876.

Inspired by Twain's own childhood,
it was the heartwarming tale
of a young boy growing up on the
Mississippi River.

Twain described it as a "hymn"
to childhood.

Illustration from *The Adventures of Tom Sawyer*, 1876

"It is a subject that is bound to stir the pulses of any man one talks seriously to about, for in this age of inventive wonders all men have come to believe that in some genius' brain sleeps the solution of the grand problem of aerial navigation."

Discussing the dream of air travel in a letter
to the San Francisco *Alta California* newspaper,
August 1, 1869

"Human nature appears to be just the same, all over the world."

The Innocents Abroad, 1869

It took Twain seven years to write his "great American novel," *Huckleberry Finn*, published in 1884.

A sequel to *The Adventures of Tom Sawyer*, it far outstripped its predecessor in scope and depth.

The story of two runaways—a white boy and a black slave—journeying down the Mississippi, the book confronted issues of race and prejudice head on.

"It's lovely to live on a raft. We had the sky, up there, all speckled with stars, and we used to lay on our backs and look up at them, and discuss about whether they was made, or only just happened—Jim he allowed they was made, but I allowed they happened; I judged it would have took too long to make so many."

The Adventures of Huckleberry Finn, 1884

"The boys dressed themselves, hid their accoutrements, and went off grieving that there were no outlaws any more, and wondering what modern civilization could claim to have done to compensate for their loss. They said they would rather be outlaws a year in Sherwood Forest than President of the United States forever."

The Adventures of Tom Sawyer, 1876

"For me its balmy airs are always blowing, its summer seas flashing in the sun; the pulsing of its surf is in my ear ... I can feel the spirit of its woody solitudes, I hear the splashing of the brooks; in my nostrils still lives the breath of flowers that perished twenty years ago."

On the Hawaiian Islands, *Mark Twain, A Biography*,
Albert Bigelow Paine, 1912

Huckleberry Finn was one of
the first novels to be written in the
vernacular—speech as spoken.

It is often hailed as the greatest
American novel ever written, though
its blunt language and treatment
of issues such as slavery and race has
also made it one of the most
banned books of all time.

"What's the use you learning to do right when it's troublesome to do right and ain't no trouble to do wrong, and the wages is just the same?"

The Adventures of Huckleberry Finn, 1884

"Damascus, the 'Pearl of the East', the pride of Syria, the fabled garden of Eden, the home of princes and genii of the Arabian Nights, the oldest metropolis on Earth, the one city in all the world that has kept its name … and looked serenely on while the Kingdoms and Empires of four thousand years have risen to life, enjoyed their little season of pride and pomp, and then vanished and been forgotten."

The Innocents Abroad, 1869

"It liberates the vandal to travel—you never saw a bigoted, opinionated, stubborn, narrow-minded, self-conceited, almighty mean man in your life but he had stuck in one place since he was born and thought God made the world and dyspepsia and bile for his especial comfort and satisfaction."

The American Vandal Speech, 1868–69

CHAPTER

FIVE

IDEAS AND
IDEALS

Whether reflecting on religion or
politics, or debating the merits of new
technology, Twain never shied away
from expressing an opinion—and was
certainly never short of words.

Works such as *Huckleberry Finn*—which
boldly took on issues such as racism
and slavery—demonstrated his talent for
combining humor and charm with
searing social commentary.

"Man is a Religious Animal.
He is the only Religious Animal.
He is the only animal that has
the True Religion—several of
them. He is the only animal that
loves his neighbor as himself and
cuts his throat if his theology
isn't straight. He has made a
graveyard of the globe in trying

his honest best to smooth his brother's path to happiness and heaven … The higher animals have no religion. And we are told that they are going to be left out in the Hereafter. I wonder why? It seems questionable taste."

"The Lowest Animal," 1910

"**O**ften it does seem such a pity that Noah and his party did not miss the boat."

Christian Science, 1907

"I am quite sure now that often, very often, in matters concerning religion and politics a man's reasoning powers are not above the monkey's."

Autobiography of Mark Twain, 2010

Twain was fascinated by technology and innovation.

As well as financing several inventions, he developed and patented three products: an elastic garment strap, a scrapbook with pre-gummed pages, and a memory board game.

The self-pasting scrapbook was the most commercially successful—more than 25,000 were sold.

"I have, as you say, been interested in patents and patentees. If your books tell how to exterminate inventors, send me nine editions. Send them by express."

Responding to an author looking to publish a book of legal advice for inventors

"Reader, suppose you were an idiot. And suppose you were a member of Congress. But I repeat myself."

Mark Twain, A Biography, Albert Bigelow Paine, 1912

"**M**an is the only slave. And he is the only animal who enslaves. He has always been a slave in one form or another, and has always held other slaves in bondage under him in one way or another … The higher animals are the only ones who exclusively do their own work and provide their own living."

The Lowest Animal, 1897

"Fleas can be taught nearly anything that a congressman can."

What is Man? and Other Essays, 1917

"We are called the nation of inventors. And we are. We could still claim that title and wear its loftiest honors if we had stopped with the first thing we ever invented, which was human liberty."

On America, Foreign Critics speech, 1890

In the 1890s, Twain struck up
a friendship with the scientist
Nikola Tesla.

Fascinated by Tesla's work
with electricity, Twain famously
took part in an experiment with an
electromechanical oscillator
(a vibrating plate) that the scientist
thought might be therapeutic.

By all accounts, the plate acted as
a strong laxative!

"Patriotism is usually the refuge of the scoundrel. He is the man who talks the loudest."

Education and Citizenship speech, 1908

"**B**efore I had chance in another war, the desire to kill people to whom I had not been introduced had passed away."

Autobiography of Mark Twain, 2010

"My land, the power of training! Of influence! Of education! It can bring a body up to believe anything."

A Connecticut Yankee in King Arthur's Court, 1889

"There is something fascinating about science. One gets such wholesale returns of conjecture out of such a trifling investment of fact."

Life on the Mississippi, 1883

IDEAS AND IDEALS

Illustration from *Life on the Mississippi*, 1883

"Man is the only animal that deals in that atrocity of atrocities, War … He is the only animal that for sordid wages will march out … and help to slaughter strangers of his own species who have done him no harm and with whom he has no quarrel … And in the intervals between campaigns, he washes the blood off his hands and works for 'the universal brotherhood of man'—with his mouth."

"What Is Man?" 1906

Twain's writing made him a great deal of money, but several ill-judged investments cost him his fortune.

Most disastrously, he attempted to create his own publishing house, and poured money into the Paige compositor, an automatic typesetting machine that promised to revolutionize newspaper production but was a flop.

In 1894, he was forced to file for bankruptcy.

"In religion and politics, people's beliefs and convictions are in almost every case gotten at second-hand, and without examination, from authorities who have not themselves examined the questions at issue but have taken them at second-hand from other non-examiners, whose opinions about them were not worth a brass farthing."

Autobiography of Mark Twain, 2010

"**A**n honest man in politics shines more than he would elsewhere."

A Tramp Abroad, 1880

"To lodge all power in one party and keep it there is to insure bad government and the sure and gradual deterioration of the public morals."

Autobiography of Mark Twain, 2010

"To be good is noble; but to show others how to be good is nobler and no trouble."

Following the Equator, 1897

A gifted public speaker, Twain was as much known for his lectures and speeches as he was for his writing.

His carefully crafted pieces, delivered with style and wit, were spoken entirely from memory.

After filing for bankruptcy, Twain's "Around the World" tour in 1895–96 allowed him to clear many of his debts.

"Honesty is the best policy— when there is money in it."

Speech, March 30, 1901

"**W**henever you find yourself on the side of the majority, it is time to reflect."

Notebook, 1904

"There is no such thing as a new idea. It is impossible. We simply take a lot of old ideas and put them into a sort of mental kaleidoscope. We give them a turn and they make new and curious combinations. We keep on turning and making new combinations indefinitely; but they are the same old pieces of colored glass that have been in use through all the ages."

Mark Twain, A Biography, Albert Bigelow Paine, 1912

"Thousands of geniuses live and die undiscovered—either by themselves or by others."

Autobiography of Mark Twain, 2010

"It takes a thousand men to invent a telegraph, or a steam engine, or a phonograph, or a photograph, or a telephone, or any other Important thing—and the last man gets the credit, and we forget the others. He added his little mite—that is all he did."

Letter to Anne Macy, *The Story Behind Helen Keller*, 1933

CHAPTER
SIX

MAXIMS AND ADVICE

In 1897, Twain summed up his idea of the perfect maxim: "A minimum of sound to a maximum of sense."

Often humorous, though sometimes tinged with pessimistic thoughts, Twain's pithy observations and sage musings seems as relevant to us today as they did more than 100 years ago.

“Wit, by itself, is of little account. It becomes of moment only when grounded on wisdom.”

Abroad with Mark Twain and Eugene Field,
Henry W. Fisher, 1922

"When angry, count four; when very angry, swear."

Pudd'nhead Wilson, 1894

"There is no character, howsoever good and fine, but it can be destroyed by ridicule, howsoever poor and witless. Observe the ass, for instance: his character is about perfect, he is the choicest spirit among all the humbler animals, yet see what ridicule has brought him to. Instead of feeling complimented when we are called an ass, we are left in doubt."

Pudd'nhead Wilson, 1894

"**I**f you pick up a starving dog and make him prosperous, he will not bite you. This is the principal difference between a dog and a man."

Pudd'nhead Wilson, 1894

Twain's final years were marred by tragedy and grief.

The death of his beloved daughter, Susy, in 1896, was followed by the deaths of his wife, Olivia, in 1904, and his youngest daughter, Jean, in 1909.

He began writing "The Death of Jean" a few hours after her death— it was, he said, "to keep my heart from breaking".

"I lost Susy thirteen years ago; I lost her mother—her incomparable mother!—five and a half years ago; Clara has gone away to live in Europe; and now I have lost Jean. How poor I am, who was once so rich!"

"The Death of Jean," *Harper's Magazine*, 1911

"Lie—an abomination before the Lord and an ever-present help in time of trouble."

Speech, March 30, 1901

"There are three things which I consider excellent advice. First, don't smoke to excess. Second, don't drink to excess. Third, don't marry to excess."

In his final address, St Timothy's School for Girls, Catonsville, MY, June 9, 1909

"**A**rchitects cannot teach nature anything."

"Memorable Midnight Experience,"
Number One: Mark Twain's Sketches, 1874

"Forget and forgive. This is not difficult, when properly understood. It means you are to forget inconvenient duties, and forgive yourself for forgetting. In time, by rigid practice and stern determination, it comes easy."

Pudd'nhead Wilson, *More Tramps Abroad*, 1897

"It is at our mother's knee that we acquire our noblest and truest and highest ideals, but there is seldom any money in them."

Mark Twain, A Biography, Albert Bigelow Paine, 1912

"Clothes make the man. Naked people have little or no influence in society."

More Maxims of Mark, ed. M. Johnson, 1927

Illustration from *The Adventures of Huckleberry Finn*, 1884

"Hain't we got all the fools in town on our side? And ain't that a big enough majority in any town?"

The Adventures of Huckleberry Finn, 1884

In the final years of his life, Twain dictated a series of musings and anecdotes that would form his autobiography.

He specified, however, that the full autobiography should not be published until 100 years after his death, in 2010.

As he wrote, he wanted to be able to speak his "whole, frank mind" without fear of giving offense.

"In this Autobiography I shall keep in mind the fact that I am speaking from the grave. I am literally speaking from the grave, because I shall be dead when the book issues from the press."

Autobiography of Mark Twain, 2010

"There is nothing comparable to the endurance of a woman. In military life she would tire out an army of men, either in camp or on the march."

Mark Twain's Autobiography, 2010

"That is just the way with some people. They get down on a thing when they don't know nothing about it."

The Adventures of Huckleberry Finn, 1884

"To die oneself is a thing that must be easy, & light of consequence; but to lose a part of oneself—well, we know how deep that pang goes, we who have suffered that disaster, received that wound which cannot heal."

Letter to Will Bowen, November 4, 1888

"There are no accidents, all things have a deep and calculated purpose; sometimes the methods employed by Providence seem strange and incongruous, but we have only to be patient and wait for the result: then we recognize that no others would have answered the purpose, and we are rebuked and humbled."

"The Refuge of the Derelicts," *Fables of Man*, 1972

"I notice that you use plain, simple language, short words, and brief sentences. That is the way to write English—it is the modern way and the best way. Stick to it; don't let fluff and flowers and verbosity creep in. When you catch an adjective, kill it. No, I don't mean utterly, but kill most of them—then the rest will be valuable."

In a letter to D.W. Bowser, March 20, 1880

"**A**dam and Eve had many advantages, but the principle one was that they escaped teething."

Pudd'nhead Wilson, 1894

Twain wrote at least 28 novels
as well as up to 100 short stories.
They ranged from humorous tales and
engaging travel literature to serious
commentaries on the issues of the day.
Ten of the best are:

The Adventures of Huckleberry Finn
The Adventures of Tom Sawyer
Roughing It
A Tramp Abroad
Life on the Mississippi
A Connecticut Yankee in King Arthur's Court
The Tragedy of Pudd'nhead Wilson
Following the Equator
Autobiography of Mark Twain
Personal Recollections of Joan of Arc

"A successful book is not made of what is in it, but of what is left out of it."

Letter to Henry H. Rogers, April 26–28, 1897

"Be good and you will be lonesome."

Following the Equator, 1897

"Let us endeavor so to live that when we come to die even the undertaker will be sorry."

Pudd'nhead Wilson, 1894

"Dying man couldn't make up his mind which place to go to—both have their advantages, 'heaven for climate, hell for company!'"

Mark Twain's Notebook, 1933

"The only very marked difference between the average civilized man and the average savage is that the one is gilded and the other is painted."

Mark Twain's Notebook, 1933

"He had discovered a great law of human action, without knowing it—namely, in order to make a man or a boy covet a thing, it is only necessary to make the thing difficult to attain."

The Adventures of Tom Sawyer, 1876

"What, Sir, would the people of the earth be without woman? They would be scarce, Sir, almighty scarce."

Speech, January 11, 1868

"When I am king, they shall not have bread and shelter only, but also teachings out of books, for a full belly is little worth where the mind is starved."

The Prince and the Pauper, 1881

Illustration from *The Prince and the Pauper*, 1881

"By what right has the dog come to be regarded as a 'noble' animal? The more brutal and cruel and unjust you are to him, the more your fawning and adoring slave he becomes; whereas, if you shamefully misuse a cat once, she will always maintain a dignified reserve toward you afterward—you will never get her full confidence again."

Mark Twain, A Biography, Albert Bigelow Paine, 1912

"Yes, even I am dishonest. Not in many ways, but in some. Forty-one, I think it is."

Letter to Joseph Twichell, March 14, 1905

"Life does not consist mainly—or even largely—of facts and happenings. It consists mainly of the storm of thoughts that is forever blowing through one's head."

Autobiography of Mark Twain, 2010